This book belongs to

_____

_____

FOR THE REAL LITTLE LUCIE OF NEWLANDS

First published in 1905

THE TALE OF
MRS. TIGGY~WINKLE

BY BEATRIX POTTER

Dalmatian Press

Once upon a time there was a little girl called
Lucie, who lived at a farm called Little Town. She
was a good little girl—only she was always losing her
pocket-handkerchiefs!

One day little Lucie came into the farmyard
crying—oh, she did cry so! "I've lost my pocket-
handkin! Three handkins and a pinny! Have *you*
seen them, Tabby Kitten?"

2

The kitten went on washing her white paws. So Lucie asked a speckled hen—

"Sally Henny-penny, have *you* found three pocket-handkins?"

But the speckled hen ran into a barn, clucking—

"I go barefoot, barefoot, barefoot!"

And then Lucie asked Cock Robin sitting on a twig.

Cock Robin looked sideways at Lucie with his bright black eye, and he flew over a stile and away.

Lucie climbed upon the stile and looked up at the hill behind Little Town—a hill that goes up—up—into the clouds as though it had no top!

And a great way up the hillside she thought she saw some white things spread upon the grass.

Lucie scrambled up the hill as fast as her stout legs would carry her. She ran along a steep pathway—up and up—until Little Town was right away down below—she could have dropped a pebble down the chimney!

Presently she came to a spring, bubbling out from the hillside.

Someone had stood a tin can upon a stone to catch the water—but the water was already running over, for the can was no bigger than an eggcup! And where the sand upon the path was wet—there were foot-marks of a *very* small person.

Lucie ran on and on.

The path ended under a big rock. The grass was
short and green, and there were clothes—props cut from
bracken stems, with lines of plaited rushes, and a heap
of tiny clothespins—but no pocket-handkerchiefs!

But there was something else—a door! straight into
the hill. And inside it someone was singing—

> "Lily-white and clean, oh!
> With little frills between, oh!
> Smooth and hot—red rusty spot
> Never here be seen, oh!"

7

Lucie, knocked—once—twice, and interrupted the song. A little frightened voice called out, "Who's that?"

Lucie opened the door: and what do you think there was inside the hill?—a nice clean kitchen with a flagged floor and wooden beams—just like any other farm kitchen. Only the ceiling was so low that Lucie's head nearly touched it; and the pots and pans were small, and so was everything there.

There was a nice hot singey smell. And at the table,
with an iron in her hand, stood a very stout short person
staring anxiously at Lucie.

Her print gown was tucked up, and she was wearing
a large apron over her striped petticoat. Her little black
nose went sniffle, sniffle, snuffle, and her eyes went
twinkle, twinkle; and underneath her cap—where Lucie
had yellow curls—that little person had PRICKLES!

"Who are you?" said Lucie. "Have you seen my pocket-handkins?"

The little person made a bob-curtsey—"Oh, yes, if you please'm. My name is Mrs. Tiggy-winkle. Oh, yes, if you please'm, I'm an excellent clear-starcher!" And she took something out of a clothes basket and spread it on the ironing blanket.

"What's that thing?" said Lucie—"that's not my pocket-handkin?"

"Oh, no, if you please'm; that's a little scarlet waistcoat belonging to Cock Robin!"

And she ironed it and folded it, and put it on one side.

Then she took something else off a clothes horse—
"That isn't my pinny?" said Lucie.

"Oh, no, if you please'm; that's a damask tablecloth belonging to Jenny Wren. Look how it's stained with currant wine! It's very bad to wash!" said Mrs. Tiggy-winkle.

Mrs. Tiggy-winkle's nose went sniffle, sniffle, snuffle, and her eyes went twinkle, twinkle; and she fetched another hot iron from the fire.

"There's one of my pocket-handkins!" cried Lucie—
"and there's my pinny!"

Mrs. Tiggy-winkle ironed it, and goffered it, and
shook out the frills.

"Oh, that is lovely!" said Lucie.

"And what are those long yellow things with fingers like gloves?"

"Oh, that's a pair of stockings belonging to Sally Henny-penny—look how she's worn the heels out with scratching in the yard! She'll very soon go barefoot!" said Mrs. Tiggy-winkle.

"Why, there's another handkersniff—but it isn't mine; it's red?"

"Oh, no, if you please'm. That one belongs to old Mrs. Rabbit; and it *did* so smell of onions! I've had to wash it separately. I can't get out the smell."

"There's another one of mine," said Lucie.

"What are those funny little white things?"

"That's a pair of mittens belonging to Tabby Kitten.
I only have to iron them; she washes them herself."

"There's my last pocket-handkin!" said Lucie.

"And what are you dipping into the basin of starch?"

"They're little dicky shirtfronts belonging to Tom Titmouse—most terrible particular!" said Mrs. Tiggy-winkle. "Now I've finished my ironing. I'm going to air some clothes."

"What are these dear soft fluffy things?" said Lucie.

"Oh, those are woolly coats belonging to the little lambs at Skelghyl."

"Will their jackets take off?" asked Lucie.

"Oh, yes, if you please'm. Look at the sheep-mark on the shoulder. And here's one marked for Gatesgarth, and three that come from Little Town. They're *always* marked at washing!" said Mrs. Tiggy-winkle.

And she hung up all sorts and sizes of clothes—small
brown coats of mice; and one velvety black moleskin
waistcoat; and a red tailcoat with no tail belonging to
Squirrel Nutkin; and a very much shrunk blue jacket
belonging to Peter Rabbit; and a petticoat, not marked,
that had gone lost in the washing—and at last the basket
was empty!

Then Mrs. Tiggy-winkle made tea—a cup for herself
and a cup for Lucie. They sat before the fire on a bench
and looked sideways at one another. Mrs. Tiggy-winkle's
hand, holding the teacup, was very very brown, and very
very wrinkly with the soap suds. And all through her gown
and her cap, there were *hairpins* sticking wrong end out,
so that Lucie didn't like to sit too near her.

When they had finished tea, they tied up the clothes
in bundles; and Lucie's pocket-handkerchiefs were
folded up inside her clean pinny, and fastened with a
silver safety pin.

And then they made up the fire with turf, and
came out and locked the door, and hid the key under
the doorsill.

Then away down the hill trotted Lucie and Mrs.
Tiggy-winkle with the bundles of clothes!

All the way down the path, little animals came out of
the fern to meet them; the very first that they met were
Peter Rabbit and Benjamin Bunny!

And she gave them their nice clean clothes. And all the little animals and birds were so very much obliged to dear Mrs. Tiggy-winkle.

So that at the bottom of the hill when they came to the stile, there was nothing left to carry except Lucie's one little bundle.

Lucie scrambled up the stile with the bundle in her hand; and then she turned to say "Good-night," and to thank the washer-woman—But what a *very* odd thing! Mrs. Tiggy-winkle had not waited either for thanks or for the washing bill!

She was running running running up the hill—and where was her white frilled cap? and her shawl? and her gown—and her petticoat?

And *how* small she had grown—and *how* brown—
and covered with PRICKLES!

Why! Mrs. Tiggy-winkle was nothing but a
HEDGEHOG.

(Now, some people say that little Lucie had been asleep upon the stile—but then how could she have found three clean pocket-handkins and a pinny, pinned with a silver safety pin?

And besides—*I* have seen that door into the back of the hill called Cat Bells—and besides *I* am very well acquainted with dear Mrs. Tiggy-winkle!)

The End